# Scarem's House

The Merry family went out, slamming the old door shut behind them, and the ghostly O'Gools were left in a state of shock.

Scarem was also furious. "My father built this house and now these humans are just going to sell it over our heads! It's already occupied! By us! Don't ghosts have any rights at all?"

**Dare you try *another* Young Hippo Spooky?**

The Screaming Demon Ghostie
*Jean Chapman*

**Three Young Hippo Magic stories to enjoy:**

The Little Pet Dragon
*Philippa Gregory*

The Marmalade Pony
*Linda Newbery*

My Friend's a Gris-Quok
*Malorie Blackman*

**Ready for a Young Hippo Adventure?**

Henry to the Rescue and Other Stories
*Ruth Silvestre*

**Young Hippo Adventures for confident readers:**

The Outfit Series –
The Secret of Weeping Wood
We Didn't Mean To, Honest!
*Robert Swindells*

Malcolm Yorke

# Scarem's House

Illustrated by Terry McKenna

Scholastic Children's Books,
Scholastic Publications Ltd,
7–9 Pratt Street, London NW1 0AE, UK

Scholastic Inc.,
555 Broadway, New York, NY 10012-3999, USA

Scholastic Canada Ltd,
123 Newkirk Road, Richmond Hill,
Ontario, Canada L4C 3G5

Ashton Scholastic Pty Ltd,
P O Box 579, Gosford, New South Wales,
Australia

Ashton Scholastic Ltd,
Private Bag 92801, Penrose, Auckland,
New Zealand

First published in the UK by Scholastic Children's Books, 1994

ISBN 0 590 55813 7

Typeset by Contour Typesetters, Southall, London
Printed by Cox & Wyman Ltd, Reading, Berks.

10 9 8 7 6 5 4 3 2 1

# Chapter 1

At the end of a humpy, bumpy track deep in the countryside there was a gloomy wood. In the middle of this wood stood a derelict house which nobody had lived in, or even visited, for many years. The house was not empty, though – it was inhabited by a family of ghosts.

There was a father ghost called Scarem

O'Gool, his wife Panic O'Gool and their twins, Gob and Lin O'Gool. Their ghost dog, Dreary, lived in a mouldy cupboard in what had once been the kitchen, and a ghost owl, called Howl, had his perch on a dusty beam in the attic.

As everyone knows, all ghosts sleep through the day because they don't like sunshine. The wood was so gloomy and the windows so dirty and cobwebby that very little light could get into the house, which made it splendidly damp and chilly for them.

All the O'Gools slept on rotten leaves on the floor. Scarem and Panic had the big bedroom, where part of the ceiling had fallen down. Gob and Lin had a smaller room, where fungus grew on the walls and toadstools came out of the spongy floorboards.

They all thought the house was lovely and creepy, and in that droopy, dismal kind of way that ghost families have, the O'Gools were quite content.

Every evening when the sun had set, they would get up and have breakfast in the dark. Of course ghosts cannot eat solid food, instead, they feed by smelling things. Favourites are a good waft of stagnant water, a sniff of mildew, the scent of mould and a pinch of rust. There were plenty of these delicious ghost foods scattered around their crumbling house.

After breakfast Gob and Lin always took Dreary for his midnight walk in the wood, where he would chase ghost rabbits and bark mournfully. At the same time Howl would glide off to hunt ghost mice in the undergrowth. For the rest of the night the family would flit around, giving the odd groan or *whoooooooo*! until the sun rose and it was time to go back to their mouldy beds.

Sometimes, as a special treat, they would all shimmer off to the churchyard five miles away, where they would spend a satisfyingly miserable hour or two moaning and wailing round the graves. On their way back through the village they might make a half-hearted effort to rattle a few doorknobs or howl down a chimney and tap on a window. Nobody in the village ever seemed to notice these things, but the O'Gools weren't bothered because they didn't want to have any close contact with humans. People were all far too cheery and noisy for the timid ghosts.

It was a very lonely, very boring and very joyless life, and they had lived like this for two hundred and fifty years.

## Chapter 2

One sunny day, the O'Gools were woken up by a creak-creak-creaking from the front door. What could it be? The twins ran straight through the wall into their parents' room and clung to them as the door creaked again. Then it slammed open! They all jumped in terror. Dreary shot up the stairs yelping with fright and Howl fluttered down through the ceiling to see what was wrong. Next they heard footsteps – human footsteps on the floorboards below. Then – horror of horrors – human voices! How the O'Gools shivered and shook.

"Of course the house needs a few things doing to it, Mr Merry," said a man's voice.

"Oh, I can see that all right!" replied another man's voice with a great booming laugh.

"Perhaps we should knock it down and start again," said a jolly woman's voice.

"I admit it's in need of repair, but of course that's why the price is so low," came the first voice again.

More doors banged and footsteps pounded downstairs, then a boy yelled, "Wow! Come and look at this cellar Joy – it's really creepy!"

"Yeah! Spooky!" a girl replied. "Race you up the stairs!" And they thundered up in spite of shouts from the house agent to watch out for the rotten steps and bannisters.

The rest of the humans came upstairs too and began to explore every room. The ghosts, remembering that humans could not see or hear them, followed, still quivering with fright.

"And we could always grow our own mushrooms in here!" observed Mrs Merry with a laugh, putting her hand on the slimy plaster in Gob and Lin's room.

"True, but try to picture the rooms with nice cheerful wallpaper and a coat of paint," pleaded the young man.

"There's plenty of fresh air, I see," chuckled Mr Merry, pointing to a huge hole in the roof. He was short and energetic-looking and had curly red hair.

"Well, yes, but a few tiles would soon put that right," said the young man, who was trying his best to sell this awful old ruin.

Meanwhile, the two children were exploring and yelling to each other.

"Cor! Gregory, come and have a sniff in this cupboard!"

"Whew! What a pong! And now come and look up this chimney – I can see the sky!"

The ghosts followed the humans back down the stairs into the kitchen, getting more and more worried with every step. Were these horrible cheery people going to come and live in their home?

"Oh, this is far too dark to cook in. We'd need to put a big window in there and knock that wall through," said Mrs Merry, pointing.

"Maybe you're right, madam, but I can recommend a good local builder who could do that with no trouble at all," the salesman said.

The tour continued through the other rotting old rooms, the children running ahead and jumping up and down on the floorboards.

"Careful, you two, or you'll drop through into the cellar where all the ghosties are!" chortled Mr Merry and everybody laughed.

"Now, sir and madam, what do you think of it?" asked the salesman when they had seen everything.

"Well," said Mr Merry. "It's certainly a challenge. It would take a lot of money and a lot of paint, wallpaper, carpets, lights, plumbing, electricity and gardening to put it right."

"And we'd need a good road and a drive to the front door so we could get the car and the furniture van here," Mrs Merry pointed out. But there was a gleam in her eye as if she would enjoy all the bustle and planning.

"And then of course the milkman could deliver our milk and the postman could bring us letters and birthday cards and all our friends could drive up and we'd have barbecues and parties," added Mr Merry.

"So will you take it?" asked the salesman hopefully.

"I think we will," Mr and Mrs Merry said together.

"Great!" yelled the children so loudly that more plaster came tumbling down from the ceiling.

"I'm so glad," said the salesman, obviously relieved to be rid of the damp old dump.

"And I think even Felicity our cat will enjoy it here with the woods to hunt mice and rabbits in," said Mr Merry as he shook hands with the salesman on the deal.

## Chapter 3

The Merry family went out, slamming the old door shut behind them, and the ghostly O'Gools were left in a state of shock.

Scarem was also furious. "My father built this house and now these humans are just going to sell it over our heads! It's already occupied! By us! Don't ghosts have any rights at all?"

"Did you hear what they said?" wailed
Panic. "Paint! Wallpaper! Carpets! Ugh! I've
kept this as a nice depressing house all these
two hundred and fifty miserable years and
now they're going to come in and spoil it all."

"Electricity!" snorted Scarem in disgust. "That means lights and radiators and those new-fangled television things we've seen in the village. Sheer vandalism!"

"And doesn't plumbing mean there'll be nasty hot water?" asked Gob.

"And what does a party mean? And what's a barbecue?" enquired Lin.

"Two revolting human children about the place laughing and playing and enjoying themselves all day – we'll never get to sleep!" Panic declared indignantly.

Dreary moaned and Howl hooted dolefully as they thought about Felicity the cat and all the troubles *she* would cause.

The ghosts were now even more miserable than usual, but this time they were not enjoying it. They sulked and drooped around the house gloomily waiting to see what would happen next.

# Chapter 4

A few days later the O'Gools heard voices and the sound of machinery nearby. When they went to look after dark they found work had begun on turning the humpy bumpy lane into a smooth road leading to the garden gate. A week later they were woken by the arrival of a car. The invasion of their home had begun.

"Well, here we are, folks! Welcome to Merry Mansion!" boomed Mr Merry as he threw all the doors and windows wide open to let the sunshine in. The ghosts gibbered in fear.

There were bangs and clatters and yells all morning and at midday Mrs Merry used a little portable stove to heat some tomato soup and pies for lunch. The sickening smell of warm food drifted through the house, making the ghosts rush outside holding their stomachs and noses. They fled to a cave in the woods and stayed there until dark.

When it was quiet enough to go back to the house, they found that Mr and Mrs Merry had repaired the roof and swept out all the rotten leaves they used as beds. All the cobwebs had gone and a fire had been lit in the fireplace. The warmth and smell of soap and disinfectant made their home seem absolutely disgusting.

Over the next few weeks the O'Gools got
very little sleep as Mr and Mrs Merry re-
plastered the walls and put up colourful
wallpaper. They replaced the rotten wood-
work and painted everything in dazzling
glossy colours. Next they put in a damp-proof
course, radiators, a washing-machine, cooker,
fridge, water heater and lights. Then came
carpets and a television. All day long Mr
Merry whistled as he worked and Mrs Merry
sang along with the music on her radio.

Outside the whole family helped cut the grass with an electric mower, planted flowers, trimmed the trees with a chain-saw, uprooted brambles and made a huge bonfire of all the rubbish.

When the Merrys' furniture arrived the white fluffy cat, Felicity, came too. She immediately chose to sleep in a new cupboard in the kitchen corner where Dreary usually slept. The ghosts retreated to the attic. It was the only place left with a bit of dust and dark.

The O'Gools were horrified at the destruction of their house. No more draughts, no more damp, no more gloom, no more cobwebs – the place was shockingly warm, light, dry, clean and, worst of all, cheerful. They huddled together in the attic and whispered through the night. Whatever could they do to get rid of these awful humans and their dreadful laughter and jolly bustle? Something drastic had to be done! And quickly!

# Chapter 5

On the evening the Merrys held their house-warming party Mr O'Gool called a family meeting.

"Somehow we've got to fight back," he declared, shaking his fist in the direction of the attic stairs. Sounds of dance music and whoops of laughter came drifting up from the party.

"Oh, this is terrible!" groaned Panic. "What'll we do, Scarem?"

"Hey, that's it, Panic!" Scarem exclaimed. "You've just given me an idea! That's what we'll do – we'll scare 'em."

"Good idea," said his wife. "After all, these humans are supposed to be frightened of us ghosts, aren't they?"

"And if we really scare them enough they'll leave, won't they?" said Gob.

"And take their disgusting wallpaper with them," added Lin.

"And their ghastly cat," muttered Dreary and Howl, who had both been badly frightened by Felicity's fierceness and the way she had taken over the wood as if she owned it.

The ghosts started to feel a bit more hopeful, especially when Scarem began to organize them.

"Now, if I remember what Grandfather O'Gool told me (and he lives in a haunted castle so he ought to know), what frightens these humans most is if you make sudden strange noises when they're not expecting them."

"And what about moving things around so they can't find them?" suggested Panic.

"Or we could let them get a glimpse of us in the distance, floating through walls and ceilings – that'll scare them," said Gob.

"They'll soon wish they'd never come!" Lin concluded with gloomy glee.

They all had a little practice at making sudden weird noises, moving things, and popping out of the plaster before they set off to haunt the Merry family. The plan was that Mr and Mrs O'Gool would tackle the parents and Gob and Lin would frighten the children. Dreary and Howl would take care of Felicity the cat.

Downstairs the party was hotting up. People were doing Highland reels in the sitting room so that when Scarem howled, "Whooooooooooooooooooooooooooooo!" it wasn't even heard.

Mrs Merry's friends were chatting to her in the kitchen while she prepared the food. Panic tried moving the knives and forks and jellies and sandwiches and drinks around to confuse them, but they were talking so hard and in such a muddle already they never even noticed.

In the hall the children were having a race to see who could pop the most balloons by sitting on them, so that when Gob and Lin banged all the doors shut to scare them nobody took the slightest notice. They all tried and tried but not one of the humans was in the least bit bothered.

At last the party was over and the guests departed. Mr and Mrs Merry flopped into armchairs to watch the late night movie on television. Panic and Scarem thought this was a good chance to show themselves. They tried waving their arms about to get noticed, and even joined hands and danced in front of the television screen.

"Reception's not very good tonight, is it dear?" said Mr Merry.

"No, too many wavy lines," agreed Mrs Merry. "Give the telly a good thump!"

Meanwhile, upstairs Gob and Lin had found the children sitting up in their beds reading books. Both were wearing headphones and listening to music tapes at the same time.

"Yaaaaaaaaaaaaaaaaaaaaaa!" shrieked Gob.

"Booooooooooooooooooooo!" howled Lin.

Neither Joy nor Gregory looked up from their books – their earphones blocked out all other sounds.

Next Gob and Lin threw some books and toys on the floor and then some of the children's clothes, but the room was already so untidy with books, toys and clothes scattered all over the carpet, that neither of the children noticed.

Down in the kitchen Felicity was asleep in her cupboard. Dreary and Howl woke her by pulling her whiskers, which made her furious.

She couldn't see them, but she puffed up her fur and spat with such rage that Dreary and Howl fled back to the attic, badly scared. There they met the rest of the baffled ghosts.

"These humans are so noisy they can't even hear our howling," said Scarem in disgust.

"Those children will never notice if we move things around because their things don't have proper places anyway. The two of them are incredibly untidy!" complained Gob and Lin.

"And none of them can see us because all this awful light everywhere shines straight through us. So now what do we do?" asked Panic, scratching her head.

"I think I'll go over to Castle Dire and see Grandfather O'Gool and ask if we can borrow some real haunting equipment – you know, skulls and chains and white sheets and that kind of traditional spooky stuff," said Scarem. "I know they use them in the castle and they've scared a lot of people there."

The others agreed. It was obviously going to take some serious haunting to get rid of this stupid family of humans.

"This means war!" declared Scarem as he melted through the floor and set off to visit Grandfather O'Gool.

## Chapter 6

The first time the O'Gools tried rattling chains outside the bedroom windows in the middle of the night, Mr Merry said, "Drat! I must have left the gate open," and got out of bed to close it.

"Funny, it was shut tight," he told Mrs Merry when he returned.

At first none of the humans seemed to

notice the ghosts floating around in white sheets, perhaps because the house was so bright they didn't show up. So Panic dyed them black and they tried again. After a few glimpses of floating black things going in and out of the walls Mrs Merry thought she needed spectacles and went to the optician's.

"It's strange, but he said my eyes were perfectly normal," she told Mr Merry.

Meanwhile, Gob and Lin were moving things around in the children's room.

"You've moved my radio from where I left it by my bed and put it in my pyjama drawer," Gregory accused Joy.

"No I never, and anyway, you've shifted my music tapes from my desk and dropped them in the wastepaper basket."

"That's not true and you know it!"

The children had a loud quarrel and after that they watched each other closely. Gob and Lin thought this was a good sign.

Down in the kitchen Felicity heard a dog barking and sharpened her claws ready to fight. She knew there were no dogs living within miles and this bark came from inside the house, so she searched and sniffed but found nothing, though she thought she saw a doggy tail whisk round the kitchen door.

Later there seemed to be an owl perched on a shelf, but when she leaped up to grab it all she did was bring the crockery tumbling and smashing down. Now Felicity was in disgrace with her humans, as well as being a very puzzled cat. Howl was very proud of this.

Mr Merry heard a long wailing coming down the chimney one night and thought it must be a strange kind of bird call. When he imitated it to a bird expert he was told there was no such thing. He was very baffled by this, especially as the next time he heard the wailing it came out of his wellington boot!

One day Mrs Merry thought she saw a human thigh bone in the vegetable rack, but when she picked it up it changed into a leek. "I really *do* need glasses," she muttered.

Once Gregory mistook his muddy football for a skull, and Joy could have sworn there was a shrunken head in the fruit bowl until she picked it up and found it was a shrivelled apple.

Mr Merry thought he glimpsed a hooded face peering over his shoulder as he was looking in the mirror to shave. He cut his chin.

One evening, the Merry family were playing a rowdy game of dominoes when they heard chains rattling upstairs. At the same time a radiator began to howl, whaaaaaa! and a hand holding a skull appeared through the wall above the fireplace and disappeared back again. A dog woofed in the kitchen and an owl hooted from the hallway, and all the doors in the house slammed shut, bang! bang! bang! one after the other. The Merrys sat up straight and looked very puzzled indeed.

"Now, that's very strange," said Mr Merry. "Just now I seemed to hear a lot of odd noises around the house – did anyone else hear them?"

"Yes, we did," they all agreed.

"And I've heard them before," added Mrs Merry.

"So have I," said Joy.

"And me," said Gregory.

Then they all recounted the peculiar things they had seen and heard over the past few days.

"I once saw a figure in a kind of black sheet follow me up the stairs," Mr Merry confessed.

"I heard an owl hoot in the bathroom, but there was no bird there and all the windows were shut," said Mrs Merry.

"I thought Joy had moved my secret diary, but it turned out that she didn't even know it existed," said Gregory.

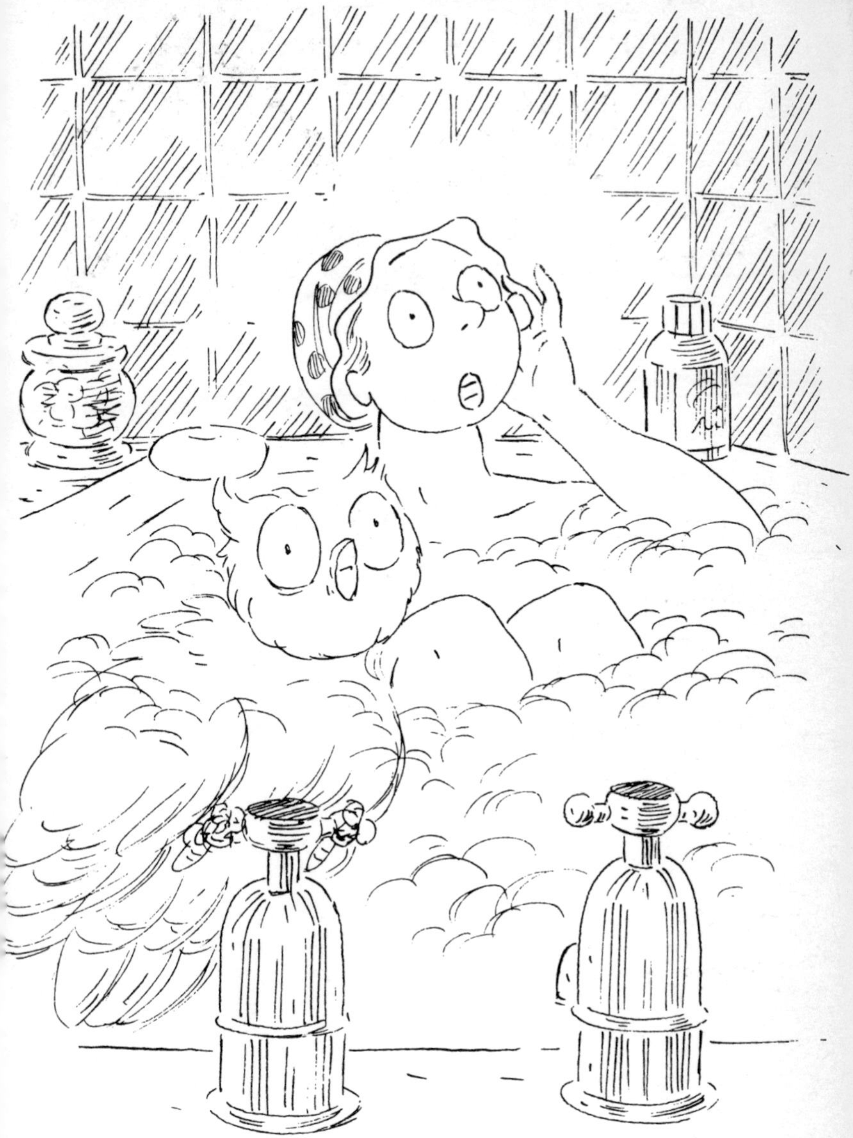

"And I thought he'd hidden all my pencils but then I found his pencils had been hidden too," said Joy.

"Well," concluded Mr Merry, "it looks to me as if there's only one explanation. We are sharing the house with ghosts!"

"Really? How very interesting!" said Mrs Merry. She was not in the least frightened.

"Wow! Great! Wait till we tell them at school!" exclaimed the children.

"Yes, this could be a lot of fun! Now, here's what we'll do, everybody," Mr Merry decided. "We'll all write down in this exercise book everything we hear and see from now on. Put the place and the time and the date as well, and at the end of a fortnight we'll see what kind of ghosts we've got. Agreed?"

Everyone agreed enthusiastically.

## Chapter 7

Each day for the next two weeks, entries like these appeared in the book:

8.30 am Thursday.
Mrs M: Saw human skull in the breadbin. Disappeared when I put my hand in for loaf.
4.30pm Friday. Mr M:
Heard dog growling in toilet. Nothing there when I opened door.

10 pm Saturday.
Joy: Saw headless figure in black sheet walking in corridor. I waved and shouted hello but it only walked up the wall and through the ceiling.

9.00am Sunday. Greg: Put my trainers under my bed last night. This morning they were floating in the washbasin.

2 am Monday.
Mrs M: Heard chains rattling
under our bed in middle of
the night. Nothing there when
I looked with torch except
some fluff. Must vacuum under
there today.
9·30 pm Tuesday. Greg:
Owl hooted in my school
bag but nothing there when
I looked.

The exercise book was left open on the sideboard and the ghosts began to read it to see if their hauntings had been noticed.

"Oh, look," said Scarem. "Mr Merry seems to have been very impressed by my scream through the letter-box."

"But not as much as Mrs Merry was by my dance of the black veils in front of the washing-machine," claimed Panic rather smugly.

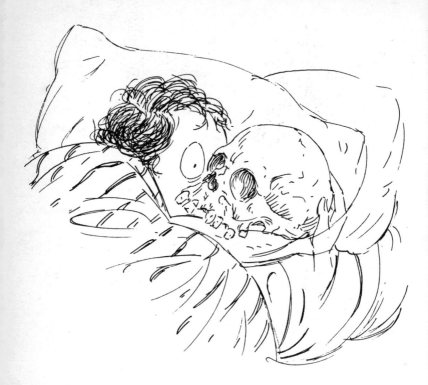

"And what about my skull on the pillow trick when Gregory woke up in the morning?" asked Gob.

"Not nearly as good as my moving the chair just as Joy was going to put her bottom on it," boasted Lin.

74

Slyly they began to compete to see who could get the most mentions in the exercise book and who could do the best haunting stunts. They even began (in a very glum kind of way, of course) to enjoy being so busy and mischievous all day and night. Because the

Merry family slept soundly they couldn't be haunted at night, so the O'Gools had to haunt them in the day, and slowly they began to get used to being awake in the daylight hours.

## Chapter 8

The Merry family showed no signs of being in the least bit frightened by all these ghostly goings on. The children began to read books about ghosts, and in their untidy way left them open around the house. The ghosts were very interested to read about other spooks, spirits, spectres, wraiths, banshees, apparitions, phantoms and hobgoblins, and all the tricks they got up to. In fact the books gave them some great new ideas to try out on the Merry family.

Then Mrs Merry began to go to the local library to find out who had lived in the old house before them. She read a lot of ancient documents and registers and made notes. When she gathered her family together to tell them all about the people who had occupied the house before them they were fascinated. So were the O'Gools, who gathered invisibly in the room listening to every word.

"Now, I've found out from the old records that this house was built three hundred years ago," said Mrs Merry.

"Really? Who by?" asked her husband.

"A family of farmers called O'Gool. They had one boy who grew up here and took over the house when his father went to work at Castle Dire."

"That's me she's talking about!" exclaimed Scarem to his family. "And Grandfather O'Gool who worked as a coachman at the castle."

Mrs Merry consulted her notes. "Then this son married a rather dismal lady from the nearby village and they had two children."

"That's me!" said Panic.

"And us!" said the twins.

"They seem to have been an ordinary kind of farming family, though they weren't very popular locally."

"Why not?" asked Joy.

"Because they were such a grumpy lot, and the other villagers thought their miserable faces could turn the milk sour."

The O'Gools all looked at each other indignantly. "Humph!" said Scarem. "Slander!" said Panic.

"Then, unfortunately," Mrs Merry continued, "there was a terrible storm. They were all in the wood gathering mushrooms, and were hit by a thunderbolt – Bang! All dead, just like that!"

"Well, I never knew that!" said Scarem.

"So that's how we went. I always wondered," said his wife.

"After that nobody wanted to live in the house because they thought it was haunted by this O'Gool family. And I think they may have been right!" Mrs Merry concluded with a laugh. The Merry family and the O'Gools, side by side, had listened with great interest and now they all gave her a clap.

Later, back in the attic, Panic said, "You know, that Mrs Merry's an interesting woman in spite of her scrubbing everything clean all the time."

"And that Joy girl has got some very interesting computer games," admitted Gob.

Scarem looked at them sternly. "Now, you two, remember these people have invaded our home. We've been here for two hundred and fifty years and I'm not giving up now! They must be got rid of! I want you all to make a bigger effort."

## Chapter 9

During the next few days, the O'Gools tried everything they could to scare the Merrys. Manacles shook, black sheets whisked in and out of rooms and the air was full of wails, toots, barks and howls. Bones seemed to be lying about everywhere and things moved almost as soon as they were put down.

The Merrys loved every minute of it.

The children began bringing friends home from school to stay the night. "Now you just listen for the dog or the owl or the chains rattling!" they'd warn their pals.

The ghosts performed more and more desperately in an effort to scare away the invading humans, so sure enough the visitors would hear a *twit-twoo!* from the wardrobe or a *woof! woof!* from behind the fridge. At night they would lie awake, thrilled to hear foot-steps dragging overhead and the clanking of metal. The windows seemed to rattle all night long and the doors slammed every few minutes even though there wasn't a draught left in the house. Joy and Gregory became very popular at school as more and more people heard about their resident ghosts.

At last Scarem called another family conference in the attic.

"Look, I'm worn out with all this flitting about and haunting stuff," he said. "I'm also running out of ideas about what to do next. Any suggestions?"

"I'm quite enjoying it," admitted Panic, "but none of it seems to be scaring them one little bit, does it?"

"I'd like to go on haunting the kitchen if you don't mind, because the steam that comes off some of the food they cook is delicious," said Gob.

"Oh, yes! Did you smell that treacle pudding they had last night? Wasn't it divine!" Lin agreed.

"I must admit I'm beginning to prefer it to the scent of mildew myself . . . but that's not the point!" said Scarem angrily. "These people have taken over our home and we have to get rid of them. Now, how can we do it? Come on – think! Panic, what do you suggest?"

"Well, they seem to have got used to all
our tricks, so what if we stopped doing
anything at all for a fortnight and see what
they'd do about that? They might just leave
out of boredom."

"Boredom? The Merrys are never bored," said Gob.

"At least doing nothing would give us time to think up some new ideas," Lin suggested.

"All right, since we don't have any other ideas we'll give that one a try. No tricks for two weeks, everybody. Agreed?"

They all agreed.

## Chapter 10

For two weeks no yowls, shrieks, whoops, clangs, boings, woofs or rattles were heard and no black wraiths or parts of skeletons were seen.

Joy and Gregory's friends were very disappointed. "I don't believe you've got ghosts at all, you're just making it up," they complained. They soon stopped asking for invitations to the house.

At the end of the first week Joy said to Gregory, "You know, I really miss all those noises and skulls and see-through figures, don't you?"

"Yes, I do. It's as if the house has gone dead. As if some friends have gone away," he agreed.

Mr Merry didn't like the quiet either. "Everything I've put down is exactly where I left it," he complained. "Screwdrivers, pencils and forks, the newspaper – absolutely nothing moves any more."

"And aren't the television programmes boring without a bit of background clatter and screeching! And I do miss seeing those

black figures nipping in and out of the walls all day long," said Mrs Merry with a sigh.

Even Felicity was bored now the owl no longer teased her by appearing and disappearing when she hunted in the wood, and the ghost dog didn't push her food dish under the washing-machine or bark in her ear when she took a snooze.

Over the evening meal they all agreed the house was a lot duller and they wished the ghosts would start their activities again.

At the end of the two weeks the O'Gools had another family conference in the attic.

"You know, I find this attic a bit chilly compared with the rest of the house," Scarem observed.

"And I'm ashamed how dusty it is," admitted Panic. "We'll give it a bit of a tidy up tomorrow."

"Fine, but that's not the point. We're here to review the battle against the Merry family," said Scarem. "Any observations? Gob?"

"It's been a very boring fortnight, and I don't think I enjoy boredom any more," said Gob.

"I agree. Flitting about in the graveyard and knocking on doors in the village is dull after you've done some real haunting," his sister agreed.

"I must admit I didn't know how to pass the time myself," Panic admitted, "so I followed Mrs Merry around. She reads some very interesting books – I had a glance through them when she put them down."

"And Mr Merry is very clever with his hands. It was quite fascinating watching him make a wooden seat for the garden," Scarem observed.

But then he remembered the Merrys were their enemies and they were still no nearer getting them out of the house. "The point is, a home once fit for ghosts to live in has been made uninhabitable!" he reminded his family.

"Well, has it, dear?" asked Panic. "After all, we *are* still inhabiting it."

"And some of those television programmes are very interesting," Gob added.

"And I've begun to understand how the computer games work by watching Joy and Gregory play them. They're great fun," said Lin.

"Felicity's really not as fierce as she looks, and I think she's a bit lonely with no other animals nearby," growled Dreary, and Howl tooted in agreement.

"What!" shouted Scarem. "Are my own family turning traitors? Don't you *want* these humans out and everything back to the lovely dreary way we had it before they invaded us?"

The other O'Gools shuffled their transparent feet and avoided his eye.

"This is terrible! Terrible!" said Scarem, stamping his foot (it went soundlessly through the floor) and storming off through the roof in a very bad temper.

"Never mind your father, dears," said Panic. "He'll be back when he's cooled down and had a think. Now shall we go down and have a sniff at the supper? I think they're having pizzas tonight followed by bread and butter pudding."

THE O'GOOLS

## Chapter 11

The Merrys were still feeling rather glum without their hauntings.

"I do hope the ghosts haven't left us for good," said Mr Merry.

"Perhaps we've offended them in some way and they're giving us the cold shoulder. If we knew what we'd done we could apologize," said Mrs Merry.

"How could we ask them to start again?" wondered Gregory.

"I bet they can read, so why don't we leave a few notes lying about inviting them to haunt us again?" Joy suggested. Everyone thought this was a good idea. They made up this letter and left several copies lying around the house:

Dear O'Grools,

It's been a bit quiet lately! We hope you haven't left us, because we had a lot of laughs when you haunted us. Would you please start again as we have missed your company.

Best wishes, Yours sincerely,
Mr Merry, Mrs Merry
Joy, Gregory
and Felicity.

The O'Gools read the notes, of course, and
Scarem called another of his family meetings
in the attic. This was now much smarter as
they'd swept the cobwebs and dust away and

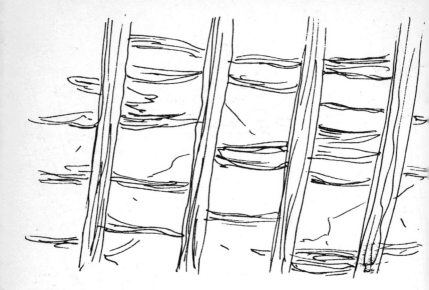

cleaned the window. It was almost as cheerful as the rooms downstairs.

"Now, what are we going to do about these notes?" he said. "I'd like to hear from you each in turn, starting with you, Panic."

"Well, I think we should go back to haunting the Merrys immediately. I realize now it will never frighten them, but I do enjoy doing it and they seem to appreciate our efforts, don't they?"

"Gob?"

"I agree. How we used to live before now looks very dull. Also I like Joy and Gregory and I'd like to make friends with them."

"Lin?"

"I think the same. It's fun playing tricks on them and their food is just delicious. I'll never

smell mildew and ditchwater ever again. Yuk!"

"Dreary and Howl?"

"Felicity's meaty chunks smell wonderful."

"And since she's been hunting in the wood there are lots more ghost mice for me to chase."

"So, you all seem to have made your minds up to live alongside these humans," observed Scarem. "Well, I've been thinking about it myself and I've come to the same conclusion. We shall never drive them out, and I'm not going to leave my home after two hundred and fifty years, so we seem to be stuck with each other."

His family cheered and clapped and howled their approval.

On the floor below, the Merrys were lying in their beds, but they sat up with big smiles on their faces when they heard the racket coming from above.

"Great! They're back," said Mr Merry and he fell happily asleep.

## Chapter 12

From that day on the two families lived alongside each other very contentedly, though one was invisible to the other.

The O'Gools still moved things mischievously, but now they also moved them to help. When Mr or Mrs Merry was working in the kitchen the O'Gools would be there sniffing all the lovely ingredients and cooking smells, but also placing in position the next wooden spoon or saucepan or herb that would be needed. In the same way, Mr Merry always found his spanners or pliers conveniently to hand when he was doing repairs on the car or the house.

Gob and Lin spent many hours playing computer games with the two human children. They still played tricks on them but the four became very good friends. At night Joy and Gregory would settle down to read in their beds while nearby two books lay on the carpet with the pages turning over by themselves.

Downstairs the four grown-ups would be watching TV together, chuckling at the same jokes or cheering for the same football team. At meals the two families were together, one inhaling the lovely warm smells of the food and the other family eating it.

The O'Gools could never speak to the humans directly but the Merrys knew they were there and addressed some of their remarks to them. Sometimes they forgot and did this when visitors were there, which baffled them.

The O'Gools always helped to blow out the candles on the birthday cakes and now they knew what a "party" meant.

They even invited Grandfather O'Gool over for a ghost party they held in the attic and he smiled for the first time in three hundred years.

In summer the two families all piled into the Merrys' old car and went off for a picnic or a day by the sea. The ghosts came to enjoy sniffing flowers, sea air, chocolate, strawberries, grass and fish and chips.

Felicity looked sleek and fit. Dreary and Howl played hide and seek with her in the woods and when they were all tired they came back home to enjoy her meaty chunks, she eating them and the other two sniffing them. Dreary and Howl now slept in her cupboard, though Felicity snored dreadfully.

The O'Gools sometimes helped to entertain guests by putting on a haunting display,

howling and wailing, shimmering and knocking on windows as they used to do. The
Merrys suggested a few new tricks they could
try. It was noticeable though that their

haunting sheets were no longer black, but a rather fashionable yellow and green floral pattern which the O'Gools had copied from one of Mrs Merry's dresses.

And the biggest change of all was that the O'Gools had at last learned to laugh.